My First Otter Book

JENNY KELLETT

BELLANOVA
MELBOURNE · SOFIA · BERLIN

My name is...

Hey there! I'm Otis the otter. Nice to meet you!

Otters are playful animals that love to swim.

Can you find me in the water?

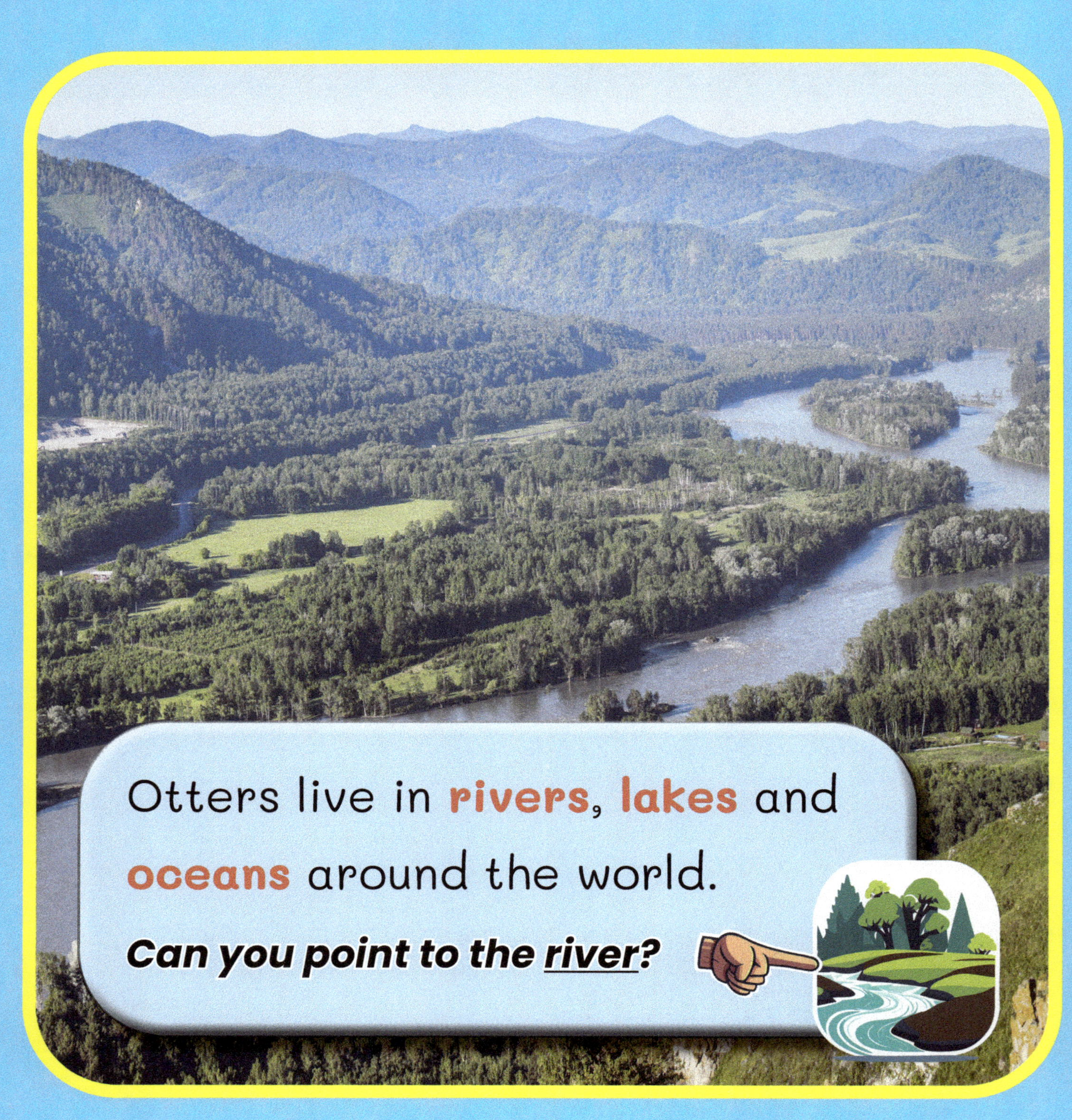
Otters live in **rivers**, **lakes** and **oceans** around the world.

Can you point to the river?

Sometimes otters play on the riverbank or beach, but they always stay close to the water.

Otters love water!
Draw a line on the map to where you think I live.
Hint: Look for the water!

Otters love to eat **fish**. They catch them with their **sharp claws**.

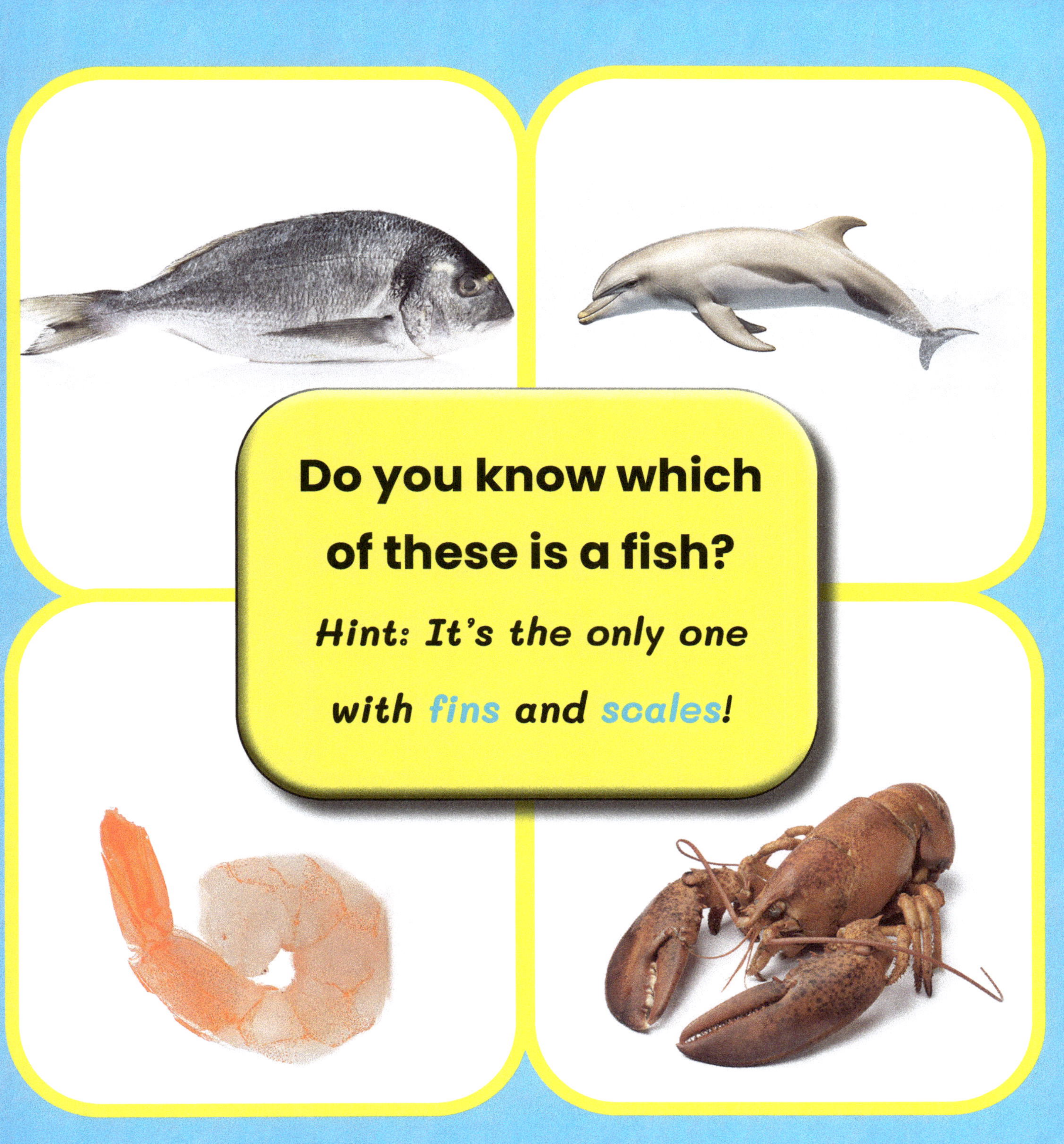

Do you know which of these is a fish?

Hint: It's the only one with fins and scales!

Otters have webbed feet that help them swim!

Which of these animals is the odd one out?

Cat

Frog

Duck

Hint: Only one of these animals doesn't have webbed feet to help them swim!

 *Point to the correct one!*

Help the otter find its way **home**!

Find the path that leads to the otter's favorite habitat.

Remember: *Otters love to live by the water!*

Sea otters live in the **ocean**, while river otters live in **rivers and lakes**.

I'm a sea otter. I have thick fur to stay warm!

Otters love to sleep while floating on their backs! They even hold hands so they don't float away.

Can you **count** how many otters there are in this raft?

Point and count each otter!

Otters are great swimmers and love to play in the water with their friends.

Let's play a
game!
Circle the animals
that like to swim!

Chirp!
Hiss!
Squeak!

Let's make some otter sounds!
Can you chirp, hiss, or squeak like an otter?!

I love spending time with my friends!
Otters are very sociable and have lots of friends. They often play and rest together.

My favorite activities with my friends...

Resting

Eating

Point to the pictures of what you like to do with your friends, too!

Swimming

Playing

Otter babies
are called
pups!
Otter moms take great care
of their pups!

Fox

Rats

Seals

Wolves

We need your help!
Otters need clean water to live.
Water pollution is a big problem for otters.

You can help
otters by keeping
beaches and rivers
clean!

What is your favorite thing about otters?

What is an otter's favorite food?

How can we help keep otters safe?

Congratulations!
Name: ....
For learning all about
OTTERS
And becoming an Otter Expert
Jenny Kellett
Bellanova Books